THE AFRICAN QUEEN

The thick forests of Central Africa are full of danger for the traveller – danger from the heat of the sun, from the millions of biting insects, from the rushing waters of the great rivers.

Rose Sayer has lived in a village in Central Africa for ten years, helping her brother in his missionary work. But then comes 1914, and the war with Germany. Soldiers come and take away all the villagers, Rose's brother dies, and Rose is left alone. So when Charlie Allnutt comes by in his riverboat, the *African Queen*, Rose packs a bag and goes with him.

Charlie is not a warlike man. His idea is to find a quiet bit of river and hide from the soldiers. But Rose thinks it would be a fine thing to take the *African Queen* down the Ulanga River to Lake Wittelsbach, and then make a torpedo to destroy the German gunboat that controls the lake. Charlie thinks this is mad. The Ulanga is full of rapids and a boat will break to pieces on the rocks in seconds. And how can he make a torpedo in the middle of the African forest?

But once Rose has made a plan, she does not give it up easily. As Charlie soon finds out . . .

OXFORD BOOKWORMS LIBRARY

Human Interest

The African Queen

Stage 4 (1400 headwords)

Series Editor: Jennifer Bassett
Founder Editor: Tricia Hedge
Activities Editors: Jennifer Bassett and Christine Lindop

C. S. FORESTER

The African Queen

Retold by
Clare West

Illustrated by
Ron Tiner

OXFORD UNIVERSITY PRESS

OXFORD
UNIVERSITY PRESS

Great Clarendon Street, Oxford OX2 6DP

Oxford University Press is a department of the University of Oxford.
It furthers the University's objective of excellence in research, scholarship,
and education by publishing worldwide in

Oxford New York

Auckland Cape Town Dar es Salaam Hong Kong Karachi
Kuala Lumpur Madrid Melbourne Mexico City Nairobi
New Delhi Shanghai Taipei Toronto

With offices in

Argentina Austria Brazil Chile Czech Republic France Greece
Guatemala Hungary Italy Japan Poland Portugal Singapore
South Korea Switzerland Thailand Turkey Ukraine Vietnam

OXFORD and OXFORD ENGLISH are registered trade marks of
Oxford University Press in the UK and in certain other countries

ISBN 978 0 19 479164 9

Printed in Hong Kong

ACKNOWLEDGEMENTS

The likeness of Humphrey Bogart on the cover is a trade mark and copyright of
Bogart, Inc. and is provided courtesy of Licensebox LLC,
a division of Moda Entertainment, Inc. www.modaentertainment.com

Word count (main text): 15,250 words

For more information on the Oxford Bookworms Library,
visit www.oup.com/bookworms

CONTENTS

1

THE DEATH
OF A BROTHER

IN A SMALL HOUSE in the African forests, an English missionary called Samuel Sayer and his sister Rose were saying their evening prayers. For the last ten years they had lived here in the German colony of Central Africa, close to the muddy waters of the River Ulanga, and far from other white men, trying to persuade the local people to accept Christianity. It was thankless work, and every night and morning it was their habit to pray, asking God for help in their difficult lives.

Rose looked worriedly at her brother. She herself was ill enough to be in bed, but it was clear to her that Samuel was much worse. He was very weak, and when he knelt down to pray, he seemed to have difficulty in getting up again. His hands were trembling violently, and in the moment before she closed her eyes to pray, Rose could see how thin those hands were, with the bones showing through the skin.

The damp heat of the African forest seemed to get even worse with the coming of the night, which closed in upon the missionary and his sister while they prayed. Rose's hands, which she was holding together, were wet with sweat, and she could feel rivers of it running down under her white cotton dress as she knelt there.

'I knew I was right to stop wearing my corset!' she thought. 'Mother always said that every woman over the age of

1

fourteen should wear one. But that's impossible here! And anyway, there's nobody to see me, except Samuel.'

She realized she should be thinking about the prayer, so she turned quickly towards her brother, making herself listen to his weak voice.

'Help us in our work, God,' he was praying.

Rose knew that this work had come to an end, now that she and Samuel were alone in the village. It was August 1914, and war was just beginning in Europe. Yesterday the German commander Von Hanneken and his soldiers had entered the village. They had taken every single person away, except the Englishman and his sister, to become part of the great German army. Now that Germany was preparing to fight against England, and Central Africa was under German control, Rose and her brother were surrounded by enemies.

'What will our life here be like now?' wondered Rose. 'Where will we get our food, oil, and matches from? How can we contact the outside world?'

She noticed that Samuel's voice was getting stronger. His eyes were shining as he looked upwards.

'Oh God,' he prayed, 'help men to see that war is not the answer to their problems. Bring them, in the end, to a lasting peace. And God, look kindly on our brave country, England. Carry her safely through this most difficult time, and give her victory over the godless ones who are responsible for this disaster!' As he finished his prayer, Samuel sounded almost like a fighting man, and Rose had never admired her brother more. Tears fell through her fingers as she covered her face

The German soldiers had taken all the villagers away.

with her hands, and bent her head. They knelt in silence for a few seconds, and then rose to their feet.

'I shall go to bed now, sister,' said Samuel quietly.

'Very well, brother,' replied Rose. She went to her own room. A little later, however, she went softly into his room in the dark, to make sure his mosquito curtains were closed.

'Good night, sister,' said Samuel. His face was very white, and he was shaking with fever.

Rose went back to her room, and lay on the bed, sweating in the terrible heat. Outside she could hear the noises of the African night. Soon after midnight she fell asleep, and woke up some hours later. She thought she heard Samuel calling, and hurried to his room.

But if Samuel had called to her, he was not conscious enough to speak clearly now. She could not understand what he was trying to say. He seemed to be explaining, perhaps to a higher being, the reasons why he had failed in Africa. He repeated the same words again and again.

'I'm sorry,' he said. 'It was the Germans, the Germans.'

He died very soon after that, while Rose cried at his bedside. After a time, she dried her eyes and slowly got to her feet. The morning sun was beating down on the forest, and she was all alone in the world.

'What will happen to me now?' she thought.

Her fear did not last long, however. Rose's thirty-three years of life, including ten in Central Africa, had made her quite self-confident. She knew that she was able to solve most problems on her own. And as she stood beside the dead man

4

in the quiet little house, it wasn't long before she stopped feeling afraid, and started feeling angry.

'Why did Samuel die?' she asked herself. 'Because the Germans broke his heart when they took all the natives away. Even if they survive the fighting, they'll lose their Christianity and go back to their old ways. That's what killed Samuel, seeing ten years of his work destroyed in a single hour!'

Since Rose was a child, her parents had taught her to love and admire her brother. When she was only a girl, he had become a missionary. She had been happy to become his helper and companion, and travel with him to this most distant and foreign corner of the world. Here she had lived and worked with him, through good times and bad, trying to learn the local languages, managing to cook meals with whatever food was available, mending and making their clothes, and visiting the villagers in their homes. Samuel had been her whole world. It was not surprising that she hated the Germans for causing his death.

And naturally, she could not see the other side of the question. Commander Von Hanneken had the difficult job of keeping Central Africa in German hands, although he knew that the real war would be fought in Europe. He only had five hundred white men in a colony of a million black people, of whom not more than a few thousand even knew they were under German control. So it was only natural that he should use every man, woman and child that he could find.

Rose remembered that she had always disliked the Germans. She remembered how unpleasantly she and Samuel had been questioned, and laughed at, when they first arrived in the colony as missionaries. She discovered that she hated the German character, their ideas, their laws, everything about them, in fact. And now that her dead brother had, in his prayers, asked God to defeat them and give victory to the English, she felt a strong wish to fight the Germans herself.

'But how can I?' she thought. 'Here I am, alone in the Central African forest, alone with a dead man. There's no possible chance of my doing anything at all.'

It was at this moment that Rose looked out of the window and saw Opportunity coming towards the house. She did not recognize it as Opportunity. She had no idea that the man who had appeared there would help her to fight for England's victory. All she realized at the time was that it was Allnutt, the London-born mechanic who worked for a Belgian gold-mining company three hundred kilometres up the river.

Samuel had disliked the man and his rough, wild way of living, and Rose did not know him at all well. But it was an English face, and a friendly one, and the sight of it made her realize how lonely she was. So she hurried outside, and waved a welcome to Allnutt.

2

THE *AFRICAN QUEEN*
GOES DOWN RIVER

ALLNUTT APPEARED VERY WORRIED, looking around fearfully all the time as he came towards her.

'Where's everybody, Miss?' he asked.

'They've all gone,' said Rose.

'Do you need any help? Where's your brother?'

'He – he's inside. He's dead,' said Rose. Her lips began to tremble, but she did not allow herself to show weakness. She shut her mouth into its usual hard line.

'Dead, is he? That's bad, Miss,' said Allnutt. He was not a brave man, and to him the missionary's death was less important than the very real danger he now found himself in.

'Have the Germans been here, Miss?' he asked.

'Yes,' said Rose. 'Look.'

He stared at the empty, silent village. 'Awful, ain't it, Miss? It was like this up at the gold mine – all the natives gone, and the Belgians too. What the Germans have done with them, God only knows. I wouldn't like to be a prisoner of that officer with a glass eye – Von Hanneken's his name, ain't it? But he hasn't got the boat, anyway. Nor what's in it.'

'The boat?' said Rose sharply.

'Yes, Miss. The *African Queen*. I was bringing back food and drink and explosives from Limbasi for the Belgians. But there's no one at the mine to take it. So it's still in the boat.'

They were inside the house now, and Allnutt, realizing that death was present, took off his sun hat.

'I'll bury your brother, Miss,' he said. The offer was rather sudden, but he and Rose both knew that in the African heat a dead man must be buried in six hours. Also, Allnutt was in a hurry to get away in case the Germans returned.

'Thank you. I'll say the prayers over his body,' Rose said, keeping her voice from trembling.

So together they carried Samuel outside, and Allnutt started digging. And when it was all over, he said, 'Don't cry, Miss. Come down to the boat. Let's get away from here.'

Rose put some things in a bag, and they followed the muddy path through the forest down to the rushing brown river. Allnutt helped Rose to climb into the boat; she sat down and looked around. The boat certainly did not look like an African queen; in fact, it was an ugly old steamboat, ten metres long, with a flat bottom, and in very bad condition.

But Allnutt seemed to know exactly how to manage it. He put wood on the fire under the boiler, and soon the engine began to make noises and send out little clouds of steam from every corner. Allnutt threw more wood on the fire, and then ran forward to the front of the boat to pull up the anchor. Then he rushed back, with the sweat running off him in rivers, put his hand on the tiller, and steered the boat out into the middle of the fast-flowing Ulanga.

'I thought, Miss,' he said, 'that we'd better find somewhere quiet behind one of these small islands, where we can't be seen. Then we can talk about what to do.'

'Yes, that would be best,' agreed Rose.

'Could you hold the tiller for a moment, Miss?' he asked.

Rose silently took hold of the tiller; it was so hot that it seemed to burn her hand. She began to enjoy feeling the boat move obediently as she put the tiller to one side or another, while Allnutt put more wood on the fire, and kept a careful eye on the river ahead. Plants grew thickly on the muddy bed

Allnutt kept a careful eye on the river ahead.

of this part of the river, and it was often difficult to find enough clear water to take a boat safely through.

'Over this way, Miss!' he called. 'That's it!'

The boat moved into a narrow channel between an island and the river's edge, where the light was all green from the leaves meeting overhead. Allnutt stopped the engine and threw out the anchor with a great crash. As the noise died away, a heavy silence seemed to close in on them.

Rose looked at Allnutt. As usual, a cigarette hung from his lower lip. He still seemed restless and jumpy, as he waved away the flies, but he was more in control of his fear now.

'Well, here we are, Miss,' he said brightly. 'Safe for the moment. The question is, what next? We've got lots of food. Two thousand cigarettes. Twenty-four bottles of gin. We've even got boxes of explosives! We can stay here for months if we want to. But do we want to? How long do you think this war'll go on, Miss?'

Rose was so surprised she could not speak. He was clearly suggesting they should stay in this hiding-place until the war was over. Did he have no wish to fight for his country?

'The trouble is,' continued Allnutt, 'we don't know which way help'll come. We don't want to get trapped here, with Von Hanneken between us and the British army. They could attack the colony from the north, south or east, though they'll find it hard getting through the forest. One thing's certain – they won't come from the west, through the Belgian Congo. The only way from there is across the lake. And nothing's going to cross the lake while the *Luise*'s there.'

10

The *Königin Luise* was the German police gunboat on Lake Wittelsbach. Its speed and its heavy gun prevented any attack on German Central Africa from the west.

'We must do something for England,' Rose said suddenly.

'Blimey!' said Allnutt. His plan had been to put the greatest possible distance between himself and the fighting, and not become involved in any way. 'Blimey!' he repeated, turning her words over in his head. The idea of 'doing something for England' was exciting, certainly. But he soon decided against it – he was a man of machinery, not of ideas.

However, he did not want to annoy Rose. 'Well, Miss,' he said, 'if there was anything we *could* do, I'd be the first to agree.' He was sure there would be nothing she could suggest.

And at first he seemed to be right. Rose was trying to remember what little she knew about war. What could two people with a boat full of explosives do to the enemy surrounding them? And suddenly she saw the light.

'Allnutt,' she said, 'this river runs into the lake, doesn't it?'

The question worried him. 'Well, Miss, it does. But you needn't think about going to the lake in this old boat, because we can't, and that's certain. Take my word for it.'

'Why can't we?'

'Rapids, Miss. Rocks and waterfalls and cliffs and white water everywhere. You haven't been there. I have. There's a hundred and fifty kilometres of rapids down that river.'

'That man Spengler, who made the first map of Central Africa, managed to get to the lake from here.'

'Yes, Miss. In a light little canoe, he was. And he had a lot

11

of native boatmen to help him. The *African Queen*'s much too wide and heavy to get through those rapids.'

All her life Rose had been used to following the advice of another person – her father, mother, or brother. Now, for the first time in her life, she was thinking for herself, and she did not find it easy, especially when it involved judging a man's character and honesty. She stared at Allnutt's face through the cloud of flies, and Allnutt, noticing her look, moved about uncomfortably. She thought of the great British Empire with its long history and its distant colonies, its beautiful warships and brave soldiers – all now in danger. She thought of her dead brother, a man of peace, who had hated any kind of fighting. But war had come at last, and had killed him with its coming. As Rose sat sweating in the *African Queen*, she knew she would do everything she could to take revenge for Samuel's death, and help her country to victory.

'Allnutt,' she said, 'with all these explosives in the boat, could you make a torpedo?'

'Could I make a torpedo? Why not ask me to build you a warship as well, while you're about it! You see, Miss . . .' And Allnutt explained in great detail why it was impossible.

But Rose was only half listening. When at last he finished, she said, 'But I think you could put some explosives in some kind of container, at the front of the boat, and then if we ran the boat against the side of a ship, we'd destroy the ship!'

'But supposing we did that, what would happen to us? We'd be dead too! And what would we want to torpedo?'

Rose was thinking unusually fast. She was not worried

about dying, and she knew perfectly well what she wanted to torpedo. But she realized she would have to be clever if she wanted to persuade Allnutt to agree.

'I wasn't thinking *we'd* be in the boat,' she said. 'We could get everything ready, then just point the boat towards the ship, and jump out at the last minute.'

Allnutt tried hard not to laugh. None of this woman's mad ideas could possibly work, but he did not want to argue, so it seemed best to agree. 'That's possible,' he said seriously.

'Good,' said Rose. 'We'll go down to the lake and torpedo the *Luise*.'

'Don't be silly, Miss! We can't get down the river. I've told you that!'

'Spengler did.'

'In a canoe, Miss, as I said, and with—'

'That just shows we can, too.'

Allnutt decided to stop arguing. She'd think differently when she saw the rapids, he thought. 'Have it your own way then, Miss,' he said. 'Only don't blame me. That's all.'

'We must start at once,' said Rose.

'What, *now*, Miss? There's only two hours of daylight left!'

'We can go a long way in two hours,' she replied, shutting her mouth tight.

So Allnutt started up the old engine, Rose took the tiller, and the *African Queen* moved slowly and noisily down river.

By the time darkness was falling, Rose was feeling pleased with herself for learning how to manage the boat so quickly.

Allnutt found a quiet place to spend the night, where leafy overhanging branches hid the *African Queen* from sight. He shut off the engine and threw out the anchor.

'Blimey!' he said, sitting down at last. 'Hot work, ain't it, Miss! I could do with a drink.' He took a bottle of gin out of one of the boxes. 'Going to have one, Miss?' he asked.

'No,' said Rose sharply. Her brother had spoken so often about the terrible effects of strong drink, but he had failed to

The water felt wonderfully cool on Rose's hot skin.

stop the natives drinking their home-made beer. Drink made men mad. Drink destroyed their bodies. Drink turned people away from God and put them on the road to hell.

But when Allnutt had drunk some gin, he did not seem to go mad or die. Instead, he said the sweetest words that Rose could wish to hear: 'What about a cup of tea, Miss?'

Tea! Heat and thirst and tiredness and excitement had done their worst for Rose. For years she and Samuel had each drunk twelve cups of tea every day, and today she'd had none. Tea! She wanted to drink ten, twenty, thirty cups of it!

'I'd like a cup of tea,' she said politely.

And after their tea, which made Rose feel warm towards the whole world, except the Germans, Allnutt said, hesitating a little, 'I'd – I'd like a bath before bedtime.'

'So would I.'

'I'll jump into the water at one end of the boat, and you can do the same at the other,' he suggested. 'Then, if we don't look, it won't matter.'

So Rose, instead of turning away from this idea in horror, found herself bathing naked in the river while a man did the same thing only a few metres away. But it did not seem to matter, and the water felt wonderfully cool on her hot skin. The forest was quiet now that it was dark, and all around her was the sound of the rushing waters of the great river.

When they were both dressed again, Allnutt made a bed for Rose with some old blankets, while he lay down nearby. The flies were biting, and Rose's head was full of thoughts crowding in. But soon, completely exhausted, she slept.

3

THE ARGUMENT

ROSE MANAGED TO SLEEP most of the night. It was the rain which woke her, the rain and the thunder and lightning. All round her was noise, with the rain beating down on the boat and the thunder crashing overhead. Rose felt the warm rain on her face, and realized she was wet to the skin.

Something moved nearby, and the lightning showed Allnutt sitting up. He looked extremely miserable.

'Blimey!' he said. 'Wet, ain't it?' For a moment Rose felt she wanted to put an arm round his shoulders and hold him like a child. She blushed secretly when she realized this, because Allnutt was no more a child than she was.

Instead, she sat up and said, 'What can we do?'

'Nothing, Miss,' he replied unhappily. 'Just wait.'

Then the storm passed as quickly as it had come. The wind died away, the sky suddenly became light, and steam rose from everything touched by the morning sun.

'What should we do before we move on?' asked Rose.

'We've got no wood. And we'll have to pump out the boat – it's full of rainwater.'

'Show me how to do that. You go and get the wood.'

So Rose was introduced to the hand pump, a tired old piece of machinery, which often trapped her fingers painfully and sometimes refused to work at all. In the end she came to hate that pump more than anything she had ever hated before. Finally, however, the boat was cleared of water, and then she helped Allnutt bring the wood onto the boat.

'We'd better start now,' said Rose.

'Breakfast?' suggested Allnutt, and then, cleverly, 'Tea?'

'We'll have that while we're going along,' said Rose.

All her life Rose had been happy to let her brother Samuel order her about. Now that he was dead, however, she had discovered that she was good at deciding what to do. She desperately wanted her plan to succeed, and she would not allow anything to delay or prevent it.

Allnutt did not mind Rose giving orders. The woman was a bit mad, he thought, but at present it would be more trouble to argue with her than to obey her. And Allnutt always avoided trouble if he could.

He started up the engine, and the boat steamed noisily back into the main channel. Soon they were travelling down river again, with Rose at the tiller. Allnutt brought some tea and tinned meat to her as she sat at the back of the boat, then he returned to keep a watchful eye on the engine.

It was hot for Rose as the sun climbed higher, but even hotter for Allnutt, working next to the heat of the fire and the boiler. She felt sorry for him, and understood why he kept drinking river water, although she knew how unhealthy it was. In fact, Allnutt was used to impossible temperatures. He had worked in ships' engine rooms where the air was far hotter than on the River Ulanga, and he was even enjoying his endless battle to keep the *African Queen*'s engine going.

Soon they were in a wider part of the river, a kilometre wide. Allnutt did not like the open water; he was afraid Von Hanneken's men were watching the river and would see the *African Queen*. Rose knew what was worrying him, but she had no fear herself. She did not believe anyone, not even Von Hanneken, could stop her now. But in order to calm Allnutt, she steered the boat across the river to the opposite bank, where she could see a long narrow island. She already knew enough about the river to know that behind the island would be the entrance to many smaller channels, where they could travel hidden safely from any watching eyes.

The boat moved out of the sunlight into the quiet water of the narrow channels. These backwaters were peaceful places, where even the birds and insects seemed to be silent in the steaming heat. There were only the tall trees along the banks, and the thick weeds waving in the dark water.

All the days they spent going down river to the rapids were like that first day. Sometimes the boat could not get through the channel they had chosen, so they had to go back and find another one. One day there were so many weeds in the water that the propeller would not turn at all, and Allnutt had to swim half-naked under the boat and cut the plants away from it. Occasionally there were storms, which caused Rose to work long and painfully with the hated hand pump.

But none of this made Rose unhappy. She was really alive now, for the first time. Life with Samuel had been one of prayer and dull routine, and she had never realized what an adventurous place Africa could be. She had her plan to think about; that in itself was enough to keep anyone happy. And the river, wide, changeable, always different, brought new excitement every day. Perhaps those few days of happiness were Rose's payment for thirty-three years of misery.

One evening, however, Allnutt was silent and appeared annoyed. Rose noticed this, and looked sharply at him once or twice. There was no friendly feeling between them as they drank their tea. And when the tea was finished, Allnutt took out his gin bottle and had a drink, and then another, still silent and angry. He drank again, and the drink seemed to

Allnutt had a drink, and then another, still silent and angry.

make him angrier. Rose was worried. She knew she must do something, because this silent drinking could only lead to trouble.

'What's the matter, Allnutt?' she asked gently.

Allnutt drank again, and stared down at his feet. Rose came nearer to him. 'Tell me,' she said.

'We ain't going further down the bloody river,' he said at last. 'We've gone far enough.'

'Not going any further!' said Rose, surprised. 'But of course we must go on!'

'There's no bloody "of course" about it,' said Allnutt.

'I can't think what's the matter,' said Rose.

'The river's the matter. And Shona.'

'Shona!' repeated Rose. Now she understood his fears.

'If we go on tonight, we'll be in the rapids tomorrow. And before we get to the rapids, we have to go past Shona.'

'But nothing's going to happen to us at Shona.'

'Ain't it? Ain't it? How do you know? If there's anywhere on this river the Germans are watching, it'll be Shona. That's where the road from the south crosses the river. And I know what the river's like there – I've been there, and you haven't. No backwaters, no islands, nowhere to hide.'

'But they won't be able to stop us.'

'Won't be able—! Don't be silly, Miss. They'll have guns, and they'll get a good view of us. They'll shoot, all right.'

'Let's go past at night, then.'

'We can't do that – the rapids start just below Shona. If we went past in the dark, we'd have to go down the rapids in the dark. And I ain't going down the rapids, not in the dark, and not in the light, either. It's bloody crazy coming so near to Shona anyway. They could find us, even *here*. Tomorrow I'm going back up river to that backwater we were in yesterday. That's the safest place for us.'

Rose was white with angry disappointment. She tried to stay calm, to explain, to persuade, but Allnutt refused to answer. Only when, in the growing darkness, Rose called him a coward – the first time she had used that word to anyone – did he reply.

'Coward yourself,' he said. 'You ain't a lady, Miss. That's what my poor old mother would say to you, if she was alive. If my mother could hear you—'

When a man who is drinking gin starts talking about his mother, he is past all argument, as Rose began to realize. She was alone in a boat with a man who was drunk – a most frightening situation. She stayed silent, ready to fight for her life or her virginity, and quite certain that one or the other would be in danger before the morning.

But Allnutt, when drunk, was neither violent nor interested in women. Mentioning his mother had brought tears to his eyes. He talked loudly and confusedly about the women he had known and his boyhood friends in London, and made a noisy attempt to sing a song. Finally, through the darkness, Rose heard the sound of a body falling heavily onto the floor of the boat, and she knew he must be asleep.

Rose, however, did not close her eyes all night. At that moment she had no hope left, and she hated Allnutt for destroying her plans. Although she desperately wanted to carry on, she knew she could not manage the *African Queen* alone. She decided, as the hours slowly passed, to make Allnutt pay for his cowardliness. Her mouth became a thin line. She would make life hell for him! Now that Samuel was dead, she had no use for kindness or goodness or any other Christian feelings.

The next morning Allnutt woke with the worst headache he had ever had. The light hurt his eyes, and he could only sit there, holding his head in his hands. Rose, meanwhile, was emptying all the gin bottles over the side of the boat. Then, without even looking at him, she made herself some breakfast. Next, she washed some clothes and hung them up to dry, still without a word to Allnutt. This was, in fact, the beginning of the great silence.

Rose had been able to think of no better way of making Allnutt's life hell – she did not realize it was the most effective way. By the end of the day Allnutt, who loved talking, was desperate for some conversation.

'Blimey, ain't it hot?' he said, coming to sit beside Rose. She said nothing. She was very busy, doing some sewing.

'Ain't you going to answer me, Miss?' he asked. 'I'm sorry about last night. It was bad to drink so much, I know. There! I don't mind saying it, Miss. And you've thrown away the gin, so I've learnt my lesson.'

But when there was still no answer, Allnutt became angry. 'Have it your own bloody way, then!' he said, getting up and going to the other end of the boat.

Rose went on calmly with her sewing, while Allnutt spent some time repairing the boiler and the engine. But when he had washed all the oil off himself, there was nothing left to do. And all round him was the silence of the river, which in itself was enough to make him feel lonely and uncertain.

Rose was emptying all the gin bottles over the side of the boat.

4

RIDING THE RAPIDS

ALLNUTT WAS NOT intelligent enough to win the battle against Rose. He was not used to doing any continuous thinking, so he was helpless in a situation where there was nothing to do except think. In the end, it was the noise of the river endlessly beating against the riverbank which defeated him.

He had tried several times to talk to Rose, and only once had he managed to make her say anything.

'I hate you,' she had said then. 'You're a coward and you tell lies, and I won't ever speak to you again.'

She was surprised to see how much he disliked her silence. She had only wanted revenge, but now she began to realize how much power she had over him, and hoped that, in the end, she could persuade him to obey her.

Allnutt was also reconsidering the situation. At first he had thought Rose was angry with him for being drunk. Then he realized her anger was at his refusal to go on down river. But her plan still seemed so wild and crazy that he made himself live with Rose's silence for another twenty-four hours.

And that was a very long day and night. Allnutt had grown up in a busy city, and all his life he had worked in crowded ships and noisy engine rooms. Silence was one of the things he could not live with. That night it even prevented him from sleeping, which was quite new for Allnutt and worried him a great deal. So, in the morning, when he thought of the awfulness of the long day ahead, he said, 'Tell me what you want to do, Miss. Just tell me, and I'll do it.'

'I want to go on down the river,' said Rose.

Once more Allnutt's head was full of terrible pictures of guns and rocks and rapids, of death by drowning, of capture by the Germans. He was frightened, but he felt he could not stay a minute longer in this backwater.

'All right, Miss,' he said. 'Come on.'

Some time later the *African Queen* steamed out of the backwater into the main river. Rose sat holding the tiller, completely happy. They were on their way again, to help England, and the thought of a little danger could only add to her happiness.

'That's the hill Shona stands on,' Allnutt called to Rose, pointing to the cliffs on their right. They had reached Shona much faster than he had expected. He looked fearfully up at the steep riverbank for any sign of soldiers or guns. Then he returned to his fire, feverishly putting on more wood, to make the *African Queen* reach its top speed.

The natives on the hill saw the boat coming, and ran to tell the German officer in the village. He hurried to the edge of the cliffs, and recognized the *African Queen* at once. Von Hanneken had given special orders to capture the boat.

'I suppose the English missionaries and the mechanic have got tired of hiding in the backwaters,' the officer thought. 'They're coming to surrender. Von Hanneken will be pleased!'

But his smile soon disappeared when he realized the *African Queen* was not coming in to surrender at all, but was going on down the river at full speed. He shouted angrily for the guards, and the natives came running with their guns. He ordered them to shoot, but they were not well trained, and none of the shots appeared to reach the boat.

'Again!' he shouted angrily. But the *African Queen* still seemed to be untouched, and was steaming fast away from Shona. He took a gun from a native, and tried to hit the boat himself. But now the distance was a thousand metres, and the sun was in his eyes.

There was nothing more he could do. He watched helplessly, as the *African Queen* moved out of sight round the bend in the river. 'The mad English will probably die in the rapids,' he thought, 'and the boat will be destroyed on the rocks! How angry Von Hanneken will be when he hears! Maybe I won't tell him – he's certain to say it was my fault.'

○ ○ ○

Meanwhile, as the *African Queen* steamed past Shona, Rose kept the boat as close to the further bank as she could. She looked across the wide river and up at the red-walled village at the top of the cliffs. It was too far to see clearly, but she could see no movement, and nothing had happened so far.

Suddenly there was a strange noise in the air, like insects in a great hurry, and then the bang of the guns. The sound echoed back from cliff to cliff.

'They've got us!' cried Allnutt, jumping up, his face white with excitement. Rose did not say anything – she needed all her concentration to keep the boat in the middle of the river now, in order to take the next bend. A moment later the whole boat rang like a bell, and two small holes appeared high up on one side. As the boat went round the bend and left Shona behind, Allnutt stood up and shouted angrily at the unseen enemy.

'Take care of the engine!' screamed Rose.

They were flying along now, because the river had become narrower and faster. Here and there were the alarming signs of rocks hidden under the water. Rose never took her eyes off the river; it was safe to go where the water was smooth, but she had to watch out for any movement in the water and decide in a second the best way to steer the boat past.

Round another bend they went, faster still. They could see rocks in the channel now, with angry white water rushing round them, coming frighteningly close. Rose saw a channel wide enough for the boat, and took it. Ahead was a long green hill of rushing water, at the end of which she could just see the top of a dangerous black rock above the water – it would cut the whole bottom out of the boat if they hit it. She kept the boat straight, and then at the last moment pushed the tiller hard to one side. The engine did its work, and the kick of the propeller forced the boat through the water, just missing the rock by centimetres.

The sound of fast-flowing water, echoing back from the cliffs, frightened Allnutt terribly, but he had no time to look about him. He knew, even better than Rose, that their lives depended on his keeping the engine going, so he bent to his

Rose rode the rapids like a queen of the sea.

work with fear in his heart. For the first time since he left school, he was saying his prayers.

It was only a few seconds before they reached the next rapid, with its ugly rocks, white waves, and hills of green water. Rose rode it like a queen of the sea. She had never enjoyed anything so much before. She was filled with the wild excitement that comes in battle, as her quick eye and lightning thought and strong hand on the tiller took the *African Queen* past danger after danger to safe water beyond.

A moment later they took another bend in the river and found themselves in the worst rapid so far. While Rose was picking a channel through the rocks, she noticed that Allnutt was waving at her. In the noise of the crashing water, he could not make his voice reach her. He held up a piece of wood and pointed to it. She understood. It was a warning that they must get more wood from the riverbank.

Rose looked desperately into the distance. Luckily, she soon saw what she wanted. Ahead, a row of sharp-looking rocks ran almost across the river, broken only in the centre, where a wall of green water had built up. Below these rocks was clear water. She aimed the *African Queen* at the gap in the rocks. The old boat crashed into the wall of water, climbed up it, then shot down the other side into the clear water beyond. At once Rose pulled on the tiller as fast as she could, and the boat came round, then shot forward again.

'Stop the engine!' Rose screamed.

Allnutt blindly obeyed. The boat turned, and came up gently and safely against the riverbank.

29

'Blimey!' said Allnutt. He and Rose looked at each other. They had escaped from the Germans, and now they had found the one bit of peaceful water in the rapids. It was unbelievable.

The place where they found themselves was cool and pleasant. For once they were away from the damp African heat, and there were no insects. Allnutt climbed on to the riverbank to collect the wood he needed, while Rose pumped out the boat. Then they sat down comfortably together, to eat a large supper and drink several cups of strong, sweet tea.

Freedom, an open-air life, and a taste of success had changed Rose wonderfully. The last ten days had taught her a great deal about her own character and Allnutt's. She had learnt to make plans, give orders, and work as hard as a man. Even her body had now filled out and she looked almost beautiful – quite different from the thin, dried-up woman Samuel had known.

By the time Rose and Allnutt had finished their supper, the excitement of the day was beginning to take effect, and their tired ears no longer noticed the crashing noise of the water all around them. They smiled happily and proudly at each other, before they lay down to sleep in their separate places. Allnutt was delighted he had survived the day, and Rose felt she had nothing more to worry about. Neither of them had any idea how much danger was still to come.

5

A NIGHT OF LOVE

THEY ALMOST FELT, next morning, that they had had enough adventures. Allnutt looked at the rushing waterfall behind them, and then at the dangerous rapids ahead, and he was frightened. It was easy to imagine the boat broken to pieces on the rocks, with Rose and himself drowning in the angry water.

But he felt a little better when he realized there was nothing to do except go on. If they stayed where they were, they would die of hunger in the end. The only possible way out lay down the river. So Allnutt put more wood on the fire, heated the boiler and started the engine. Rose took the tiller, and the old boat moved out of its quiet resting-place into the main channel. The next moment it was flying at top speed down the river, and the madness of the day had begun.

Rose seemed to be able to think like lightning, and took the *African Queen* through the rocks and the white water like a trained boatman. Later, when they had come to the end of their journey, she found she could not remember the details of that second day among the rapids with half the clearness of the first. She could see every rock, every bend of her first rapid again, just by closing her eyes. But the second day became confused with the third, and the fourth; by then she had got used to the noise and excitement and danger.

31

But the enjoyment of it all remained. She loved it when the *African Queen* hit the waves of the rapids with a great crash. And the best feeling of all was when the boat reached the top of one of those long steep hills of green water, and went rushing down with danger on each side and possible death waiting for them at the bottom.

In the afternoon they came to a wider part of the river, where there were no more rapids, although the water still flowed very fast. Now there was time for Rose to think and to enjoy herself, while making sure the *African Queen* took the bends safely. Even Allnutt did not feel he needed to concentrate so hard on the engine, and he lifted his head. Open-mouthed, he watched the steep cliffs rush by, with a feeling of horror which was almost enjoyable.

Soon Rose started looking for a place where they could drop anchor and spend the night. She noticed that another river joined the Ulanga a little way ahead, not in any normal way, but by rushing down a cliff and falling twenty metres into the water below. As she steered round this waterfall, she suddenly saw a place where the water had eaten away at the rocky riverbank. She gave a sign to Allnutt to go more slowly, then backwards, and the *African Queen* came gently to a stop under the steep bank. Allnutt tied up the boat, while Rose looked around her.

'How lovely!' she said. They had found what must be one of the most beautiful corners of Africa. The cliffs here were not so steep, and there were shelves in the rock where blue and purple flowers were growing, making the whole rock face a misty blue. Sunlight gave colour to the dancing water. The noise of the waterfall was not deafening; it sounded like music. There was no dust; there were no flies. It was no hotter than an English summer day.

Rose stood by the tiller and drank in the sweet loveliness of it all. There was further happiness in remembering the dangers they had just passed. She knew that, by bringing the *African Queen* down those rapids, she had really achieved something. For once in her life she could feel proud of herself, and she was almost drunk with a feeling of power.

Allnutt came closer to her. 'Would you mind having a look at my foot, Miss?' he asked. 'I got a splinter in it yesterday, and I ain't sure if it's all come out.'

'Of course,' said Rose.

He sat down next to her, and started taking off his shoe, but Rose knelt in front of him and did it for him. She took his rather nice-looking foot into her hands. She found where the splinter had entered the foot, and pushed with her fingers to make sure it had completely gone.

'No, there's nothing there now,' she said, and let his foot go. It was the first time she had touched him since they had left the village where Samuel was buried.

'Thank you, Miss,' said Allnutt. He stayed in his seat, staring up at the flowers, while Rose remained on her knees at his feet. 'Blimey, ain't it pretty!' he added. His voice was only just loud enough for Rose to hear above the sound of the river.

Neither of them was thinking clearly. Both of them felt

33

strangely happy with each other. But something seemed to be missing. Rose watched Allnutt's face as he looked around in wonderment. There was something attractive, almost childlike about him, which made her feel she wanted to put her arms around him. Both of them were breathing harder than usual.

'That waterfall,' said Allnutt hesitatingly, 'reminds me—'

He never said what it reminded him of. He looked at Rose, her sweet face close to him. He, too, was feeling wonderfully alive. He put his hand on her neck, sunburnt and cool. Rose caught at his hands, to hold them, not to push them away. He knelt down and their bodies came together.

Rose realized he was kissing her. The blood was rushing through her body and her head was swimming. His hands pulled at her clothes, and she could not refuse him even if she wanted to. She put her arms round his thin body and held him to her, while they made love.

It was not really surprising. Everything had pointed to it – their lonely situation, their closeness, the dangers they had survived, their healthy life. Even their arguments had helped.

Rose was made for love; in the past she had been afraid of love and avoided any thought of it, but it was impossible not to think of it, surrounded by the wild beauty of the Ulanga. She wanted to give, and to give again, and to go on giving – that was her character.

The most important thing, perhaps, was what she had been taught about men all through her girlhood. Her mother, her aunts, all the married women she knew, thought men were careless and untidy, unable to cook a meal or clean a room. These ladies explained to Rose that women had to spend all their time clearing a path for men in life, but at the same time, men were like gods, and must be loved and obeyed.

It was impossible not to think of love,
surrounded by the wild beauty of the Ulanga.

So Rose did not expect the man she loved to be perfect. She accepted that he would not earn her admiration. She would not love him so much if he did. Allnutt's weaknesses – his fondness for gin and his fear of personal danger – made him more attractive to the motherly side of Rose's nature. As the flame of passion died down in him, and, with his lips on hers, he whispered a few sleepy words to her, she was very happy, and held him in her strong arms.

Allnutt was very happy, too. His need was just as much for a mother as for a lover. There was a happiness in Rose's arms he had never known before. He felt he could depend on her as he had never depended on any woman in his life. All the misery of his past dropped away from him as he laid his head on her warm shoulder.

It was late morning when they woke, to the calm light of day. There was a moment, earlier, when Rose had blushed, ashamed at the thought of last night's passion, but Allnutt's lips were close to hers, and her fears and worries disappeared as she caught him to her. She blushed again when she had to tell him she did not know his name, and when he told her, she repeated 'Charlie' to herself like a schoolgirl.

When she felt a powerful need for the morning cup of tea – and after a night of love she needed it just as much as after a long day of riding the rapids – it was she who got up and prepared breakfast. She had not minded Allnutt preparing the meals when he was just her assistant, but it seemed wrong that Charlie (whom she already called 'husband' to herself) should have the trouble of it.

But although she was happy to do these little things for him in a wifely way, there was no question of him taking control of the *African Queen* and the journey down river. Both Rose and Allnutt knew that what had happened that night would make no difference to their plans or their daily routine. Fortunately, Allnutt had no wish to give orders, only to obey them. So he collected fresh wood as usual, and when he had got up steam, waited for Rose's command.

Only when they were about to leave did he whisper to her, 'Give me another kiss, old girl.'

And she put her arms round him and kissed him, saying softly, 'Charlie, Charlie, dear Charlie.' She looked round at the beautiful place where she had given him her virginity, and her eyes were wet. Then they untied the boat, and a second later they were in the mad rushing of the Ulanga once more.

There were more rapids to ride, and surprisingly they survived every danger, although it was too much to hope their luck would hold. They came to a place where the channel was narrow and there seemed to be no clear water at all between the rocks. Rose did her best, but as the *African Queen* shot through the white water, there was a crash under the boat.

'We've hit something!' shouted Allnutt. 'Got to stop!'

The boat was now shaking under Rose's feet and there was something terribly wrong with the propeller. Desperately, Rose searched the river for a backwater. Then she saw a very small one behind a large, flattish rock near the riverbank.

'Charlie!' she screamed, pointing to the rock.

He understood, and made the engine go faster, praying that the propeller would not pull the bottom out of the boat.

Steering had become almost impossible, and when they reached the rock, the boat tried to climb it, then began to turn on its side, and a green wave of water came right over it.

It was Allnutt who saved the situation. He jumped into the water with a rope, pushed the boat off the rock, then jumped on to the rock like a cat, pulling hard on the rope so that the boat slowly came round into the backwater.

'Blimey!' he said, when he climbed back onto the boat. 'That was close! I thought the boat was going over!'

Rose managed to smile bravely at him; she was feeling a little sick now that the danger was over.

'We'll have to pump out the boat,' said Allnutt, 'before we can find out the damage underneath.'

'I'll do that,' said Rose. 'You sit down and rest.' Pumping out the boat was the next best thing to cleaning a room. Naturally, it was not the kind of work a man should do.

Then Allnutt took his clothes off and swam under the boat. He reappeared after a minute.

'Did you see anything, dear?' asked Rose worriedly.

'Yes,' said Allnutt. It was as bad as he had feared. 'The shaft's all bent. And the propeller's got a piece broken off.'

But Rose had no idea of the awfulness of the disaster.

'We'll have to mend it, then,' she said.

'Mend it?' Allnutt laughed miserably.

He looked up at the cliffs. They were not too steep here, and he and Rose would be able to climb up to the top. Then

38

they would have to walk around in the forest until the Germans found them – or until they died of hunger.

'Don't know why the shaft didn't break in two,' he said.

'Never mind, dear,' said Rose. 'Let's have some dinner, and then we can talk about it.'

It was the best possible advice. Allnutt felt much better with a meal and plenty of strong sweet tea inside him.

Rose returned to the attack. 'What do we have to do before we can go on?' she asked.

'Well, *if* we could pull this old boat out of the water, and *if* we had a team of workmen to do the repair, and *if* we could order a new shaft and propeller from the boat's makers, and *if* the post arrived here, then we could do the repair, and go on, with no problems at all. But we can't do any of that.'

Rose knew nothing at all about anything mechanical, but she was completely confident that Allnutt would be able to solve the problem. 'Could you take the shaft off underwater?' she asked. 'And then straighten it before putting it back.'

'I'd need a very hot fire for that,' said Allnutt doubtfully. 'And then there's still the broken propeller.'

'Well, you'll have to mend that, too,' said Rose brightly. 'I'm sure you can, Charlie.'

Allnutt thought about how to mend a broken propeller with a bit of old metal in the middle of the African forest. Then he laughed at the idea, laughed and laughed, so that Rose had to laugh with him. For a moment they forgot the seriousness of their situation. They found themselves in each other's arms – how, neither of them could remember – and they kissed as two people do the day after their wedding.

Rose was so full of hope, and so sure that Allnutt could do it that in the end he agreed to try. He put his doubts to one side, and they started almost a week of back-breaking, and

It was a week of back-breaking and dangerous work.

for him, dangerous work. He had to swim under the boat to take off the shaft and propeller. When he had managed this, they heated up the shaft in the hottest part of a wood fire, so that he could change its shape by hitting it with a hammer. This job took three days, and by the time the shaft was straight enough, they were both exhausted and sunburnt.

There remained the problem of the propeller. In the end Allnutt used part of an old boiler to repair it. The cliffs rang with the sound of his hammer. Rose kept the fire going, and held bits of hot metal, burning her fingers again and again. They were as happy as children on holiday, and every new difficulty brought them closer together.

At last, another three days later, Allnutt was able to put both the shaft and propeller back in place under the boat. He had done his best, but he knew he would only find out how good his work was in the middle of the rapids and waterfalls, where death would be certain if his repairs failed.

The night before, they had both imagined this situation, and neither had wanted to mention it. They had lain in each other's arms, each terribly afraid of losing the other. They still did not discuss the danger today, as they prepared to leave.

'Goodbye, dearest!' said Allnutt, bent over the engine.

'Goodbye, dearest!' said Rose at the tiller.

Neither of them heard the other, or was supposed to; there was great bravery in them both.

The *African Queen* steamed out into the channel. Shaft and propeller held together, and the next moment they were flying down river once more, towards the white water ahead.

6

THE WAY
TO THE LAKE

SOMEWHERE ALONG THEIR JOURNEY that day they passed the place where the River Ulanga changes its name and becomes the Bora. The place is marked on no map, for the simple reason that no map of the country has ever been made, except for Spengler's confused drawings. Until he and his native boatmen managed to get their canoe down the river, no one had known that the big, fast Ulanga, which flows through most of the colony, is the same river as the small, slower Bora, which disappears in the great delta on the edge of Lake Wittelsbach.

The Ulanga, travelling at its usual breakneck speed, carries bits of wood, rocks, and mud along with it. As soon as it reaches flatter land, where it becomes the Bora, it drops all this, and separates into hundreds of tiny channels which flow into the delta. This delta has been built up over the years by the mud left behind by the river. It is a dull, swampy place, half black mud and half water, steaming in the African heat, thick with fast-growing weeds, and alive with millions of biting insects.

Rose and Allnutt soon noticed the difference between the two parts of the river. They left the cliffs behind and entered a shallow valley, with thick forest on both sides of the river. They had passed their last rapid now, and the river was much deeper and slower. But Rose still needed to concentrate on the water ahead, looking out for floating rubbish like branches, which could damage the propeller. The heat was terrible, and the sweat ran down their bodies. There were sudden storms, and then as soon as the rain stopped, mosquitoes came in a great cloud, hungry for blood. At night they did not need to search for a backwater – they just put the anchor down in the middle of the channel – but the heat and the insects made it almost impossible to sleep.

'Well,' said Allnutt one evening, as they were sitting down to eat their meal, 'we did it, old girl. We got through the rapids all right. But we wouldn't be here now if it weren't for you. Don't you feel proud of yourself?'

'No,' said Rose, almost crossly. 'Of course not. It was you who did it. Look at the way you made the engine go. Look how you mended the propeller. It wasn't me at all.'

Rose really meant what she said. She was actually beginning to forget the time when she had to use her power over Allnutt to make him continue the voyage. But she was also forgetting because she wanted to forget. Now that she had a man of her own, it seemed unnatural to her that a woman should make plans and give orders. Victory would be Charlie's achievement, not hers.

Darkness fell, and the water was like black glass all round them. They were both silent, as the boat moved gently under them, and they watched the stars come out.

'Blimey!' said Allnutt, his head on Rose's shoulder. 'Ain't it lovely?'

Rose agreed. But even in this perfect peace, there was war in both their hearts. Rose's wish to clear the lake of England's enemies burned as high as ever. Every now and then she thought with quiet happiness of the boxes of explosives packed away in the boat. Charlie would do what was necessary with them when the time came – that was a man's job. As she imagined him making an effective torpedo, she was filled with a rush of love, and put her arms round him.

Allnutt himself had no ideas of his own left. He was happy to have someone to admire and follow. Rose's complete fearlessness in the wild rapids had deeply moved him. He was now quite sure that she knew best, and was ready to follow her into any mad adventure she chose. And no other woman had been so loving and gentle to him in all his life. He could forget all thoughts of himself and his troubles while he was with her. He held her more closely, to remind himself that she loved him, and they kissed in the starlight.

The next day they steamed on down the black river in the breathless heat. It was misty, and as Rose steered round another bend, she noticed how thick the mist was becoming. It was hard to see if there were any more bends ahead, but calmly she kept to the middle of the river. Soon she began to realize that the river was much wider, and the boat was much further from both banks, than before.

Now she could not see a good channel anywhere. She decided to steer to one side, close to the dark green forest and the reeds, hoping that a channel would appear there.

'Do you think this is the delta, dear?' called Allnutt.

'I don't know,' said Rose. 'I'll tell you soon.'

But by the end of that long, tiring day, it was clear they had been steaming in a circle, because they ended up where they had begun, still with no sign of a channel. In fact, they were in a small lake, into which the Bora flows, just behind the delta. It was not surprising that Rose had not found a way out to the delta, because all the channels are narrow, and hidden by reeds and water plants, as they soon discovered.

They started very early the next morning, and Rose steered close to the reeds, searching for a channel. Twice she saw narrow openings and decided against them, but the third opening was wider and she steered the boat into it. The reeds on both sides became thicker and thicker, and then the *African Queen* seemed to hesitate. Allnutt quickly shut down the engine, fearful of damaging the propeller again.

'We're in the mud,' he said.

'I know that,' said Rose sharply, 'but we've got to go on.'

Allnutt got out into the water and tried to pull the boat along behind him, but the mud soon became too deep and too soft and he had to climb out again.

'We must pull the boat along by the reeds,' said Rose.

And that is what they did. Allnutt used the boat hook, and Rose her hands, to pull the *African Queen* along. It was terribly hot work among the reeds. And soon the insects found them again; they came in clouds until the air was thick with them, mad with the thirst for blood. The work was heavy and tiring, too. Two hours of it left Allnutt breathless.

'Sorry, dear,' he said at last. 'I must have a rest.'

Allnutt tried to pull the boat along behind him.

'All right,' said Rose. 'Give me the boat hook.'

Allnutt was too exhausted to argue. He lay, sweating, in the bottom of the boat, unable to speak. It did not take long for Rose to become completely exhausted, too. She dropped down beside Allnutt.

'We'll go on tomorrow,' she said, with difficulty. When she felt a little stronger, she stood up and looked ahead. She could see nothing except reeds and sky. How far they had come, how near they were to the delta, she could not guess. There was nothing to show they would ever get through at all. But that did not matter. They would go on trying tomorrow.

That night there was no need to throw out the anchor, as the boat lay immovable in those tall reeds. Rose and Allnutt did not feel the wind that came with that night's storm, but they were delighted with the rain.

'It'll deepen the water in our channel,' said Allnutt, as they sat in the boat, with rain beating down on their heads.

'It can't rain too much for me,' said Rose.

The next morning they were up early, looking hopefully around them. It was now clear that they were in some kind of waterway leading through the reeds. True, it was an extremely narrow line, along which the reeds grew only a little less thickly, but surely it must lead somewhere.

'I think we're floating,' said Allnutt happily, as he put the boat hook into the water to check the water level.

They continued yesterday's work, pulling the boat along by the reeds, until suddenly Allnutt gave an excited shout.

'There's another channel here!'

It was perfectly true. The new channel was wider and freer from reeds, and the water in it was actually moving.

'Look out, old girl!' said Allnutt. 'It'll be rapids next!'

They could still laugh.

Allnutt pulled the boat into the channel, and the *African Queen* moved slowly but noticeably along. A little later, Rose caught sight of trees straight ahead, two hundred metres away. Without warning, the reeds came to an end, and the channel opened out into a little lake, which was covered with pink and white water-lilies. On the far side of the lake were dark trees, growing in wild, fantastic shapes.

'That's the delta all right,' said Allnutt.

'There's a channel over that way,' said Rose. 'Look!'

Across the lake was a small opening in the line of dark trees; they could see water-lilies growing in the entrance.

But it was not easy to get across to that channel. They still could not use the engine because the water was thick with weeds, and the water-lilies were no help for pulling the boat along. Allnutt put the boat hook down into the mud and tried pushing the boat along, but the water-lilies were so thick that they made any movement very slow.

'Can't we try paddling?' suggested Rose.

'Why not?' said Allnutt. The boat had a canoe paddle, which he gave to Rose, while he used a long, flat piece of wood. Paddling the boat along gave them a little more movement, but it was extremely hard work.

They moved so slowly that it was some time before they realized they had stopped moving forward at all.

'It's that old propeller,' said Allnutt. 'It's caught up on some weeds, I expect.'

'Yes,' said Rose. 'What can we do?'

'Only one thing for it,' said Allnutt. 'I'll have to go down and cut it free.'

Rose knew there was danger for him in that deep water and thick weed, but he had to take the chance if they wanted to continue the voyage.

'You'll have to be careful,' was all she could say.

He found a piece of rope and tied it round his waist. 'You count thirty from the time I go under, and if I ain't coming up by then, you pull the rope, and go on pulling.'

'All right,' said Rose, sounding uncertain.

Allnutt was not too sure about it himself. He was rising to an unbelievable level of bravery in what he was doing. Not even Rose could guess at the sick fear inside him, but he made himself jump in. Rose began to count with trembling lips, and at 'thirty' she pulled on the rope. With a delighted smile she saw Allnutt come up, and helped him pick the weed off his face.

It took him four attempts to clear all the weed from the propeller, but when he climbed back into the boat he gave a cry of horror. All over his body and arms and legs were leeches, twenty or more of them, digging into his skin. They were horrible things, full of his blood. Allnutt was more frightened of them than anything else on this hellish journey.

'Can't you pull them off?' he cried. 'The bloody things!'

'Salt gets them off,' said Rose, and rushed to find the salt

49

tin. She put damp salt on the leeches' bodies, and they fell off, one by one, on to the floor of the boat. Rose threw them all over the side, and helped to clean Allnutt's wounds. But even when it was all over, he was still trembling with horror.

'Let's get away from here,' was his only answer to Rose's worried questions.

They paddled on through the carpet of water-lilies. It was a lovely sight, but neither of them had eyes for its beauty. All afternoon they pulled at their paddles in complete silence, in the burning heat, until they could manage no more. They put down the anchor and spent the night where they were.

In the morning they could see they were only a short distance away from the channel, so they fought their way through the hated lilies with renewed hope. They reached the mouth of the channel, and looked into it. It was deep and dark; mangrove trees grew on both sides and their branches met a few metres over the water, keeping all the sunlight out. A smell of dying plants filled the air, and the water was dark green and thick with a new kind of weed, like long grass.

'We ain't going to be able to go under steam here,' said Allnutt. 'The propeller'll never go round in those weeds.'

Rose looked at the dark, ugly mangroves. She knew it would be difficult to find another channel. It did not take her long to decide. 'Come on, then,' was all she said.

They started paddling again, and the *African Queen* moved slowly into the mangrove swamp. As the trees closed round them, they could see nothing ahead of them except an endless mangrove forest. The black mud in which the trees grew was half water, and the air was heavy with dampness. Everything was wet, and it was so hot that it was hard to breathe.

'Shall I try the boat hook now, Rosie?' suggested Allnutt.

'Can you make another hook? Then I can use one, too.'

'That'll be easy,' said Allnutt. Rose was fortunate in having an assistant like him. And a few minutes later he passed her a metal hook he had made, tied to a long piece of wood.

With both of them using hooks, the boat began to move a little faster. They stood side by side at the front of the boat; there was almost always a mangrove branch to hook on to, and help pull the boat along.

But there were other problems. Every few hundred metres the bottom of the boat hit something – usually a piece of tree hidden in the deep black water, lying right across the channel. Sometimes, if there was enough water, they could float the boat across. At other times, they managed to pull the boat through the mud around the piece of wood. And if all else failed, they had to move the piece of wood itself.

It was a terrible time of dirt and mud and bad smells. They could not prevent the mud covering everything on the boat and themselves, and with the mud came its sickening smell. Worse than anything else, it was a place of malaria. They had probably first caught it in the early part of the Bora, but it was in the delta that they first fell ill. Rose regularly gave herself and Allnutt medicine for malaria, which was probably the reason they did not die of it. Every morning they both had to lie down; their heads ached, they felt a dull coldness, and then their bodies shook helplessly.

51

They lay side by side in the bottom of the boat, shaking with cold in the steaming heat, with the silent mangroves all around them. Then at last the fever came, and with it the pain and the thirst, until finally they started sweating and the fever died away. After an hour's sleep, they woke up, able to move about once more, able to continue their work of getting the *African Queen* through the delta to the lake.

They never saw the sun when they were in that swamp, and they lost all count of time there. Days came and went – how many, they never knew. They did not eat much, and what they ate smelt of the swamp before they got it to their mouths. It was a worse life than an animal's.

They did not notice the first hopeful signs. The channel they were in was like any other channel, and when it joined another one, it was only what had happened a hundred times before. Then the branches over their heads became thinner, letting in more light; the channel was deeper and wider. When real sunlight reached them, Allnutt could wait no longer.

'Rosie,' he said. 'Do you think we've got through?'

Rose hesitated before she spoke. 'Yes,' she said at last. 'I think we have.'

They managed to smile at each other across the boat. They were awful to look at, although they had become used to each other. Their hair was covered in mud, their deeply browned skin had turned an unhealthy yellow, and their bodies were terribly thin. They still smiled at each other, all the same.

Then the channel took another turn, and in front of them was a view in which there were almost no mangroves.

They lost all count of time in that dark mangrove swamp.

'Reeds!' whispered Allnutt happily. 'Reeds!' He knew about reeds, and much preferred them to mangroves.

Rose was looking out over the reeds as far as she could. 'The lake's just the other side,' she said. At once she started to plan. 'How much wood have we got?'

'About enough for half a day.'

'Not enough – we need more than that,' she said. She knew that on the lake it would be harder to find wood. There was only one thing she would ask of the *African Queen*, but the old boat must be as well prepared as possible for it.

'Let's stop here and get some,' she decided.

Both of them, now that they had seen the blue sky and the wide water ahead, were filled with a passionate wish to get away from those hated mangroves immediately. But they knew they had to be sensible.

As Allnutt tied the boat to a mangrove and cut off some of its branches, he realized that their journey was very near its end, and that end would be the torpedoing of the *Königin Luise*. He had never believed they would get this far, and now they were here, he would soon have to think about it. But for the moment he had not a thought in his head. And when he had finished cutting the wood into smaller pieces, they were able to leave the mangrove swamp at last, for the safe and pleasant channel through the reeds.

7

THE END OF THE
AFRICAN QUEEN

IT WAS A WIDE CHANNEL, and as soon as they turned a
corner, the endless view of the lake opened out in front of
them – golden water as far as the eye could see, broken only
by two or three islands with trees growing on them. There
were reeds in shallow water on both sides of the boat, but that
did not matter. There was clear water in front of them, sixty
kilometres wide and a hundred long, with not a rock nor a
water-lily nor a reed nor a mangrove to prevent them from
steaming ahead. They both had a delicious feeling of
freedom, and that night, anchored among the reeds, they
slept more peacefully than they had for days.

And in the morning they still did not discuss the torpedoing
of the *Königin Luise*. Rose liked to complete one step before
thinking about the next. 'Let's clean the boat,' she said. 'I
simply can't make plans if there's dirt all around me.'

Indeed, in the bright sunlight the dirt in the *African Queen*
was perfectly awful. Bit by bit they washed the whole boat,
and then their clothes. In that hot sunshine things dried
almost while you looked at them. Rose got herself clean,
too, for the first time since they had entered the mangroves,
and enjoyed once more the feeling of a fresh clean dress on a
fresh clean body.

That afternoon, while looking out over the lake, Rose

saw something – something more than water and reeds and sky and islands. It was not a cloud; it was white, with black smoke coming from it. Rose's heart beat violently.

'Charlie, come here,' she called. 'What's that?'

One look was enough for Allnutt. 'That's the *Luise*. Yes, that's them all right. The bloody Germans!'

'They're coming this way!' cried Rose. 'They mustn't see us here. Can we get far enough into the reeds to prevent them seeing us?'

She made herself stay calm. The *Königin Luise* would not be able to see them yet, as the *African Queen* was too far away and much smaller than the German gunboat. She watched it carefully. It was steaming southwards along the edge of the lake, and it would be an hour before it reached the mouth of the Bora and could see the *African Queen* against the reeds.

'Let's get the boat into the reeds now,' she decided. They pushed and pulled with the boat hooks, until half of the *African Queen* was in the thick reeds.

'How deep is the mud? Can you get over the side and cut some of those reeds down?' asked Rose.

Allnutt looked doubtful as he pushed the boat hook into the mud. 'Hurry up,' said Rose sharply, and Allnutt took his knife and went over the side. In mud up to his chest, he cut every reed near him as low as he could manage. He climbed back in, and Rose pulled the boat further into the reeds.

'They'll still be able to see the back end of the boat,' said Rose. 'We need to be further in. Once more will do it.'

Allnutt silently dropped back into the water and went on

56

cutting. This time it was enough, and the *African Queen* was now well hidden from the lake by a thick line of reeds.

Rose and Allnutt watched the *Königin Luise* from their hiding-place. It looked beautiful in its white paint against the deep blue of the water. They could see the German flag flying in the light wind, and the heavy gun which gave the Germans complete control of Lake Wittelsbach.

There was clearly no danger of discovery. The ship was making a tour round the lake, checking that all was well.

'Look, they're going a different way now!' said Rose

They watched the Königin Luise *from their hiding-place.*

suddenly. The gunboat was now moving towards the islands which they could see straight opposite them.

'They ain't looking for us, then,' said Allnutt. 'I think they're stopping there for the night.' Darkness was beginning to fall, and they could only just see the ship coming to a stop close to one of the islands.

'Why weren't we ready for them today?' said Rose angrily. She blamed herself for missing the opportunity of attacking the German ship.

Allnutt lit a cigarette, and then said something surprisingly helpful. 'Don't worry, Rosie. I've been thinking. They'll come here again, I'm sure. You know what Germans are like – they always do things regularly, at certain times. They'll be back here in a week's time, just you wait and see.'

Rose felt happier at once. If the *Königin Luise* came back to these islands another time, then – her plan was made.

'Charlie,' she said, and her voice was gentle.

'Yes, old girl?'

'You must start preparing the torpedoes. Tomorrow morning, as soon as it's light. How long will it take?'

'I can put the explosives into containers quite quickly. Then I've got to find a way of detonating them – that's more difficult. Then we'll have to cut holes in the side of the boat, to put the torpedoes in. It'll take two or three days.'

'All right.' Rose's voice sounded unnatural.

'Rosie, old girl,' said Allnutt. 'Rosie.'

'Yes, dear?'

'I know what you're thinking about doing. You needn't try

to hide it from me.' He took her hand in the darkness. 'You want to take the *African Queen* out at night next time the *Luise*'s here, don't you, old girl?'

'Yes.'

'I think it's the best chance. We ought to be able to manage it.' Allnutt was silent for a second or two, preparing what he wanted to say next. 'You needn't come, old girl. There ain't no need for us both to – to do it. I can manage it myself.'

'Of course not,' said Rose. 'That wouldn't be right. I was planning to take the boat on my own.'

'I know,' said Allnutt, surprisingly. 'But—'

It was a strange argument. By now Allnutt was perfectly ready to throw away the life that had once seemed so valuable to him. Rose's plan had become like a living thing to him, or perhaps a much-loved piece of machinery. There would be something wrong about leaving it incomplete. He tried to argue that for him there would be almost no danger – he would jump off the boat at the last minute.

It all ended in their agreeing that both of them would go. Their best chance of success lay in having one person to steer and one person to take care of the engine. They also agreed that, when they were fifty metres from the gunboat, one of them would jump into the water with the life belt (they only had one). Allnutt thought they had decided it was Rose who would do the jumping, and Rose thought it would be Allnutt.

Rose was so sure of the rightness of her plan that nothing else mattered, not even keeping Charlie safe. Victory over the Germans was far more important than their own lives. She stood up in the darkness, and looked over the lake. She could see a group of distant lights.

'That's them all right,' said Allnutt.

Without those lights, Rose realized, she and Allnutt would never be able to find the *Königin Luise* on a dark night. How lucky that the Germans were confident they had no enemies on the lake to hide from! The success of her plan now seemed almost certain, and in a wild kind of happiness she turned to Allnutt. In all the uncertainty of future danger and all the certainty of future victory, she held him passionately. Her love for him and her passion for her country were strangely confused, as she kissed him in the moonlight.

○ ○ ○

In the morning the *Königin Luise* steamed off northwards.

'We'll be ready for them next time,' said Rose.

'Yes,' said Allnutt.

With Rose's help he lifted two long gas containers up from the bottom of the boat. He let the gas out, and took out the nose-fittings, leaving a hole in the end of each container. Then very carefully he opened the boxes of explosives; inside were fat sticks of yellow material, covered in oiled paper.

'We don't want them to move around in the containers – we need something to pack them in with,' he said, looking around. 'Ah yes! Mud's just the thing.' He bent over the side of the boat, picked up several handfuls of black mud and put it on the floor of the boat to dry off in the sun.

'I'll do that,' said Rose, when she realized what he wanted. She collected more mud, dried it, and carried it to Allnutt when it was ready. Bit by bit he filled the containers with the explosives, packing the mud carefully round them.

'That's good,' he said proudly when he had finished. 'Now the detonators.' From a small cupboard he brought out a hand gun. Rose stared at the weapon in great surprise.

'Sometimes I used to have to take gold to Limbasi for the company,' he explained. 'But I never had to shoot anybody.'

'I'm glad to hear it,' said Rose. To shoot a thief in time of peace seemed a much more unpleasant thing than to destroy a whole ship in time of war.

He broke open the gun and took out the bullets, and Rose watched the idea taking shape under his hands. It was a slow business, because meals and sleep and malaria took up a lot of time. But in two days Allnutt had used the bullets to make detonators, which he would put into the containers when they were ready to start. There were three bullets for each container, so there was a good chance that one would explode. Just one container would destroy the *Königin Luise*.

Finally Allnutt made two holes at the front of the boat, just above the water. Then they pushed the containers into the holes until their noses were half a metre in front of the boat.

'Well, old girl,' he said. 'We've done it all now. We're all ready. We'll just have to wait for them to come back.'

Everything they had done – coming down the rapids, escaping the Germans at Shona, mending the propeller, paddling through the weeds and the delta – all this was for just one thing, which they would soon attempt. It was a frightening thought. There was nothing to do now, and they both had a strangely empty feeling as they looked ahead to their last few days of life.

To pass the time, they worked on repairing the boiler and the engine, to make sure the boat could reach its top speed. Allnutt got into the mud under the boat, and checked the propeller. Every few minutes one or other of them looked out over the reeds for the *Königin Luise*. They were not sure how many days had passed since the Germans' last visit, and in their blackest moments they began to doubt if they would ever make their plan work.

Then one morning they looked out over the lake and saw, just as before, the white of the gunboat's paint and the blackness of its smoke. They watched it steam southwards, and then return to anchor among the islands that evening. Allnutt had guessed the Germans' movements correctly.

They turned away from watching the ship and found themselves holding hands and looking into each other's eyes. Each of them knew what the other was thinking.

'Rosie, old girl,' said Allnutt, 'we're going out *together*, ain't we?'

'Yes, dear,' said Rose. 'I'd like it that way.'

They would stand the same chance, side by side, when the *African Queen* drove its torpedoes into the *Königin Luise*. They could even smile at the thought of dying together.

It was almost dark now, and there was no moonlight.

'We can get ready now,' said Rose. 'Goodbye, dear.'

'Goodbye, dearest,' said Allnutt.

They pushed the boat out of its hiding-place in the reeds.

Then Allnutt got into the water, and with great care fixed the detonators into the noses of his home-made torpedoes. There was a wind blowing now, as he lit the fire and waited for steam to appear from the boiler. He started the engine, and the propeller began to turn. Rose stood at the tiller, and steered the boat into the lake. They were off now, to do their best for their country and their empire.

Because it was so dark, they could not see the thick clouds building up in the sky, and because they had no experience of lake conditions, they did not know how dangerous a wind from the north could be. They had no idea of the speed with which it could change calm water into mountainous waves.

Rose had had her training in rivers. She knew rocks and rapids and weeds, but she did not know the danger of taking a flat-bottomed boat like the *African Queen* into a storm on a lake. She had no fear, no fear at all, even when the boat was thrown this way and that way in the wild water, and waves began to crash over the side of the boat.

Suddenly lightning cut through the darkness and showed them the wild water all around them. Thunder followed, then came the rain, and with it, an even stronger wind. Wave after wave came crashing into the boat. Blinded by the rain and the waves, Rose fought with the tiller but was nearly knocked off her feet. Allnutt rushed back to help her, and put her arm through the life belt. Then, as the boat moved suddenly, he was taken from her. She tried to call to him, but there was no reply. She felt cold water round her waist. A wave hit her in the face; she could not breathe.

The *African Queen* went down, and the brave attempt to torpedo the *Königin Luise* for England failed. As the old boat disappeared under the waves, the storm died away and soon the waters of the lake were once more smooth and calm.

Rose fought with the tiller, and Allnutt rushed back to help her.

8

BACK TO A
WIDER WORLD

THE PRESIDENT OF THE COURT, who was the captain of the *Königin Luise*, looked at the prisoner with interest. He decided there was nothing special about the man's face – it was one that could pass quite unnoticed on a Berlin street any day of the week. He looked tired and miserable, and was clearly a sick man.

The first officer was asked to speak. He explained that the man had been found on one of the islands, and when arrested, could give no reason for being there. He was probably British, possibly a spy, and in the first officer's view they should put him to death immediately. Then the president turned to the second officer, who was supposed to speak for the prisoner. But this officer did not have much to say.

So the president of the court turned hopefully to the prisoner himself. He wanted to find out more about him.

'What's your nationality?' he asked in German. Allnutt looked at him stupidly. 'Belgian?' asked the president. 'English?'

'English,' said Allnutt. 'British.'

'What did you – were you doing on the – the island?' asked the president, trying to remember his English.

'Nothing,' said Allnutt. He was too tired and confused to understand exactly what was happening. Nothing mattered much any more, now that he had lost Rosie and the old *African Queen*. He was ill, and he almost wished he was dead.

It was difficult for the president. The punishment for spying was death. He did not want to have this man killed, but what else could he do?

Suddenly there was a noise outside the door, and a native sailor entered, pulling along with him a new prisoner. At the sight of her the president rose politely to his feet, because the prisoner was a woman, and clearly a white one. She was very thin, her hair was wildly untidy, and her clothes were dirty and full of holes.

The sailor explained they had discovered the woman on another island, and, with her, something else. He showed the court a life belt, which had the name *African Queen* on it.

'*African Queen*!' repeated the president to himself, trying to remember where he had heard the name before. Quickly he looked through the papers on his desk, and found the message Von Hanneken had sent him about the missing steamboat on the Ulanga. He looked again at the woman, and saw how exhausted she looked.

'A chair!' said the captain, and the second officer jumped up to offer the one he was sitting in. The captain had already guessed that these people must be the mechanic and the missionary's sister; they had probably left their boat on the Ulanga, come down in a canoe, and tried to cross the lake to the Belgian Congo. He began to question Rose, and was delighted to find she could speak a little German.

It came as a great surprise to him when he learnt that Rose

and Allnutt had brought the *African Queen* down the rapids of the Ulanga and through the Bora delta. He had heard from Spengler's own lips what the rapids and delta were like.

'But madam, it was very dangerous,' said the captain. ¯

Rose did not reply. Nothing mattered now. Although she had been glad to see Charlie safe, even her love for him seemed to be dead, now that the *African Queen* was lost and the *Königin Luise* still controlled the lake.

The captain knew there could be no question now of putting anyone to death for spying. He could not possibly have a woman put to death, especially one who had brought a steamboat all the way from the Ulanga to the lake. He stared at her in admiration.

'But why,' he asked, 'didn't your friend here tell us that?'

Rose looked round at Allnutt, who had now fallen to his knees, exhausted and feverish with malaria. This touched the motherliness in Rose. She went to him at once and knelt in front of him, her face full of love.

'He is ill and tired,' she said, looking round accusingly. 'He ought to be in bed.'

The captain said to his officers, 'The court is over. Leave us,' and they jumped up to obey his order. He thought for a moment. He should, of course, simply send these two to a German prison for the rest of the war. But they were ill, and perhaps they would die there. It was not right that two people who had achieved so much should die in enemy hands. Von Hanneken would be angry when he heard about it, but, after all, the captain of the *Königin Luise* could do what he liked

Rose went to Allnutt at once and knelt in front of him.

on his own ship. And in no time at all he had decided exactly what he was going to do with his prisoners.

Several hours later, in the small town of Port Albert in the

Belgian Congo, on the western edge of the lake, a British commander was preparing for an attack on the *Königin Luise* the next day. He felt hopeful that it would be successful, because for the first time he had two small, but extremely fast motorboats with powerful guns. These boats had been sent out from England, and then brought all the way overland, by railway and river.

The commander was by the lake, watching his men fix the guns onto the motorboats, when he suddenly saw a white shape, with black smoke coming from it. As he looked, a young officer came running.

'That's the *Königin Luise*, sir,' he said, breathlessly. 'And it's flying a white flag, sir.'

The commander was thinking fast. Were the Germans surrendering? Or was it a clever plan to enter Port Albert under a flag of peace and destroy his motorboats?

But it soon became clear that the Germans wanted a meeting. 'I'll go,' said the commander to the young officer. 'If anything goes wrong, just shoot. Don't worry about me.'

The officer watched as a small boat took the commander out to the *Königin Luise*. A short time later, the boat returned, and the *Königin Luise* steamed away into the distance.

He ran down to meet the commander, and was greatly surprised to see a woman and a man lying in the bottom of the boat. Both of them looked feverish and exhausted.

They were carried to the commander's office, where he questioned them. He was annoyed; he had quite enough to do, organizing an important attack on the Germans, without having to take care of a couple of sick people who had lost their boat. And Rose and Allnutt had no useful information about the Germans that he did not already know.

'How did you get down to the lake, anyway?' he asked.

'We came down the Ulanga River,' said Rose.

'Really? I didn't know it was possible to do that.'

'It ain't,' said Allnutt. 'Blimey, it ain't.'

But the commander was not really interested in their adventures; he had his own problems to worry about. And both Rose and Allnutt felt uncomfortable with these officers in their white uniforms and their coldly polite voices.

They were sent to sleep in separate houses, both feeling they had nothing left in life to look forward to.

The next morning, as the *Königin Luise* steamed over the lake it had controlled so long, the German captain saw two long grey shapes rushing towards him. He ordered his men to get the ship's gun ready, but the gun pointed forward, and the British motorboats, which could move and turn much faster than the *Luise*, were already attacking from behind.

Holes began to appear in the sides of the *Königin Luise*. When the boiler was hit, a cloud of steam surrounded the ship at once, and in that moment the mechanics in the engine room were boiled alive.

The British commander ordered his motorboats to move further away. When the steam cleared, he could see the *Königin Luise* was floating helplessly in the water. He looked for a sign of surrender, but could see none. Then something hit the water beside his boat, and he realized that the *Luise*'s officers were shooting at them. He did not want to kill the Germans, but he had to keep his own men out of danger, so, unwillingly, he gave another order. More shots rang out from the motorboats' powerful guns, killing several of the German officers. They did not hit the captain, who had gone down into the burning steam of the engine room to do what he had to, in his last moments of life.

Then the British guns stopped, and the commander looked at the *Königin Luise* again, with its German flag still flying. The ship now seemed lower in the water, and then suddenly it fell over to one side. The captain had let the water into the engine room, to prevent the ship falling into British hands.

'I hope we can save them,' said the commander, calling for full speed. The motorboats came rushing up just as the German flag, the last thing to disappear, went below the water. They were in time to save all the living except the hopelessly wounded.

○ ○ ○

There is great happiness in victory, even when a commander has so much to do – sending wounded men to hospital, writing detailed reports for London, and making sure he has enough food and bullets for his men. Now he also had wounded German prisoners to take care of, as well as the mechanic and the missionary's sister. He ordered Rose and Allnutt to come and see him in his office.

'A group of Belgian officers are taking some prisoners to the west coast today,' he told them coldly. 'I'm going to send you with them. That'll be all right with you, I suppose.'

'I suppose so,' said Allnutt dully. He did not know what to think. Even hearing that the *Königin Luise* was destroyed had made his feeling of hopelessness worse.

'You'll join the army, I expect,' said the commander. 'You'll find the British on the coast, at Matadi. They'll probably send you to fight in South Africa.'

'Yes, sir,' said Allnutt.

'And you, Mrs – er – Miss Sayer, isn't it?' the commander said to Rose. 'You can get back to England from Matadi.'

'Yes,' said Rose.

'That's all right then,' said the commander, pleased that he was solving one of his problems. 'You'll start in two hours.'

It was hard to expect an officer planning battles in a country half the size of Europe to take any more trouble over two unimportant people. It was that 'Mrs – er – Miss' which really decided Rose's future. When they left his office, she felt angry, and ashamed of being unmarried. He had mentioned the possibility of a return to England; to Rose that meant poor streets and corsets that hurt and aunts who ask too many questions. And it was terribly painful to think of losing Allnutt. Even if her feelings towards him had changed, she could not imagine a future without him.

'Charlie,' she said, 'we've got to get married.'

'Blimey!' said Allnutt. He had not thought of that.

'We must do it as quickly as we can,' said Rose. 'As soon as we get to the coast, to Matadi . . .'

Allnutt was not yet used to the idea of joining the army, and now this! He thought about Rose and her fearlessness.

He thought about money – he would receive a soldier's pay, of course. He thought about the girl he had married and left twelve years ago – she was probably with some other man by now. Oh well, South Africa and England were a long way away from each other, and she wouldn't trouble him much.

'All right, Rosie,' he said. 'Let's do it.'

So they left the lake and began the long journey to Matadi and marriage. Who can tell if they lived happily ever after or not?

GLOSSARY

achieve to succeed in doing something; **achievement** *(n)*

admire to have a very good opinion of someone; **admiration** *(n)*

ain't *(non-standard)* isn't, aren't, am not

anchor *(n & v)* a heavy piece of metal attached to a rope and dropped over the side of a boat, to stop the boat moving

assistant someone who helps

attack *(v & n)* to start fighting or hurting someone

attractive pleasant to look at

blimey *(old-fashioned slang)* a word used to express surprise

bloody *(adj & adv)* a swearword, used for emphasis, often angrily

blush *(v)* to become red in the face

boiler a container in which water is heated in a steam engine

canoe a light narrow boat moved along by paddles

capture *(v & n)* to catch and keep someone a prisoner

channel a narrow waterway

Christianity the religion based on the teachings of Jesus Christ; **Christian** *(adj & n)*

colony a country governed by people from another country

concentrate to think hard about what you are doing and not about anything else; **concentration** *(n)*

corset old-fashioned, long, tight underwear for women

court when a judge (or a person acting as a judge) asks questions and decides if there has been a crime

coward a person who is not brave when there is danger

damp a little wet

delta an area where a river has divided into many small channels

detonate   to make something explode; **detonator** *(n)*

empire   a group of countries ruled by a king or emperor

explosives   something that can cause an explosion, as in a bomb

float *(v)*   to stay on the top of water, and not sink

gin   a strong, colourless alcoholic drink

hammer   a heavy tool used for hitting things

hell   some people believe that bad people go to hell when they
    die; **hellish** *(adj)* very bad

hook   a curved or bent piece of metal

leech   a small worm found in water, which holds on to a
    person's body and feeds on their blood

life belt   a large ring that floats, used to help someone who has
    fallen into water, to prevent them from drowning

malaria   a disease that causes fever, caused by a mosquito's bite

mangrove   a tropical tree that grows in mud, with roots that
    grow down from its branches

mining   digging for gold in the ground

missionary   a person who is sent to a foreign country to teach
    people about Christianity

mosquito   a flying insect that bites and sucks blood

mud   soft, wet earth; **muddy** *(adj)*

naked   not wearing any clothes

native   a person who was born in a particular place, country, etc.

opportunity   a chance, the right time for doing something

paddle *(n & v)*   a long piece of wood with a flat end, used for
    moving a small boat through water

passion   a strong feeling, especially of love

power   the ability to control people or things

pray   to speak privately to God; **prayer** *(n)* speaking to God

propeller   a thing joined to a boat's engine, which turns round
    fast to make the boat move

pump *(v & n)* to push water out of a boat by using a machine

rapids *(n)* a place where a river flows very fast, usually over rocks

reed(s) a tall plant like grass that grows in or near water

rush *(v)* to go very fast

shaft a long piece of metal that joins parts of an engine together

splinter a small thin sharp piece of wood

steam *(n)* the hot gas that water changes into when it boils

steam *(v)* (of a boat) to move using power produced by steam

steer to guide a boat in a particular direction

surrender *(v)* to stop fighting and allow yourself to be caught

swamp an area of ground that is covered with water

sweat *(v & n)* to lose water from your skin when you are hot or afraid

tiller a handle used for steering a boat

torpedo *(n & v)* a kind of bomb that travels underwater

victory winning a battle or a war; success in a game, an argument

virginity the state of being a virgin (a person who has never had sex)

weed a wild plant

ACTIVITIES

Before Reading

1 **Read the introduction on the first page of the book, and the back cover. What do you know now about the story? Choose T (True) or F (False) for each of these sentences.**

1 The *African Queen* is the name of a steamboat. T / F

2 The story takes place in North Africa. T / F

3 Charlie agrees to Rose's plan at once. T / F

4 Rose wants to torpedo a German gunboat. T / F

5 Charlie is Rose's brother. T / F

2 **Can you guess what happens in the story? Choose one of the three possible endings to complete each sentence.**

1 The *African Queen* . . .

   a) is broken to pieces in the rapids.

   b) goes down in the lake during a storm.

   c) is attacked by a German gunboat.

2 The crew of the German gunboat . . .

   a) are killed by Charlie's torpedoes.

   b) take Rose Sayer and Charlie Allnutt prisoner.

   c) shoot Charlie as a British spy.

3 Rose and Charlie . . .

   a) get married in the end.

   b) fall out of love, and soon forget each other.

   c) are separated by the war, and never meet again.

ACTIVITIES

While Reading

Read Chapters 1 and 2. What do we know about Rose and Allnutt so far? Use these words to complete the passages.

admired, advice, afraid, agree, angry, arguing, educated, experience, good, learner, mechanic, persuade, rough, self-confidence, strong, unmarried, weak

Rose was the _____ sister of a missionary. She _____ her brother and always followed his _____. When he died, at first she felt _____, but her _____ soon returned and she began to feel _____ with the Germans. She was a woman of _____ character and was a quick _____, and soon realized that she could probably _____ Allnutt to do what she wanted.

   Allnutt was a _____ from London. He lived a _____ kind of life and was not well _____, but he was very _____ with machinery and engines, and had a lot of _____ of African rivers. He had a _____ character and did not like _____, so he thought it was best to _____ with Rose's plan for a while.

Before you read Chapter 3 (The argument), can you guess what happens? Choose one possibility for each sentence.

1 The argument is about *Allnutt's drinking / Rose's plan / work on the boat.*
2 The argument lasts for *one / two / three* days.
3 In the end *Allnutt / Rose / nobody* wins the argument.

Read Chapters 3 and 4. Choose the best question-word for these questions, and then answer them.

What / Who / Why

1 . . . didn't Allnutt mind Rose giving the orders on the *African Queen*?
2 . . . was the argument about?
3 . . . was the first to use the word 'coward'?
4 . . . did Rose do the morning after Allnutt got drunk?
5 . . . was the first to say 'sorry'?
6 . . . did Charlie finally agree to Rose's plans?
7 . . . did the German officer think when he saw the *African Queen* coming towards Shona?
8 . . . were Rose and Charlie so pleased with themselves, when they stopped by the riverbank?

Before you read Chapter 5, what do you think the 'danger still to come' is? Choose some of these ideas.

1 There are several more rapids, and in one of them the *African Queen* hits a large rock.
2 The German officer at Shona sends some of his men in canoes to catch Rose and Charlie.
3 Rose and Charlie are bitten by mosquitoes and become seriously ill with malaria.
4 Rose and Charlie are attacked by Africans, who think they must be Germans.
5 Wild animals come out of the forest one night, and attack Rose and Charlie while they are asleep in the boat.

Read Chapters 5 and 6, then match these halves of sentences.

1 Although Rose and Charlie had become lovers, . . .

2 The shaft and the propeller were very badly damaged, . . .

3 When Rose and Charlie set off again down river, . . .

4 In the delta the water was thick with weeds and roots, . . .

5 At last they came to the end of the mangrove swamp . . .

6 they both said a secret goodbye to each other.

7 and knew that they had succeeded in reaching the lake.

8 they both knew they would still continue with the plan.

9 which meant they had to pull the boat along by hand.

10 but Rose was confident that Charlie could mend them.

Before you read to the end of the story, can you guess what happens? Choose any of the ideas which go together.

1 The *African Queen* . . .

    a) sinks in a storm on the lake.

    b) is badly damaged by German gunfire.

    c) manages to torpedo the German gunboat.

2 Rose and Charlie . . .

    a) are both drowned in the lake.

    b) are caught and shot by the Germans.

    c) decide to get married in Africa.

3 The *Königin Luise* . . .

    a) destroys several British ships on the lake.

    b) chases the *African Queen* out of the lake.

    c) is destroyed by British gunboats.

ACTIVITIES

After Reading

1 **Perhaps this is what some of the characters in the story are thinking. Match the characters to the thoughts, and say what has just happened in the story at this moment.**

Rose, Charlie, Samuel, the British commander at Port Albert, the German officer at Shona, the captain of the Königin Luise

1 'I can't believe they're surrendering! Have they heard about the motorboats, I wonder? No, they've been well hidden. They can't be planning . . . No, it must be something else.'

2 'Right, that's the last one. Perhaps that'll teach the little coward a lesson. And I won't say a word to him all day . . .'

3 'My God, they've got away! They'll be round the bend in a minute. Crazy people. They'll be killed in the rapids for sure. I think I'll just forget I ever saw the boat go past . . .'

4 'I've always tried hard, I've always done my best. Now I must leave everything in God's hands, and take myself to bed. I'm too weak to do any more . . .'

5 'That's it – no chance of getting away now. I've got to get down to the engine room. At least I'll make sure they don't get the boat – it would be too useful for them.'

6 'What's this? Oh God! It's horrible! And there's another – and another! There's hundreds of them, all over me!'

2 **Perhaps there was a newspaper reporter at Matadi, who interviewed Rose about her adventure. Complete Rose's side of the conversation.**

REPORTER: So, Miss Sayer, you and Mr Allnutt left the village and set off down the Ulanga. Go on with your story.

ROSE: _____.

REPORTER: An argument? What was that about, then?

ROSE: _____.

REPORTER: So you went on and got past Shona. Then you were in the rapids. Weren't you frightened, Miss Sayer?

ROSE: _____.

REPORTER: The propeller? But how did you manage to fix it in the middle of the forest?

ROSE: _____.

REPORTER: Well, Mr Allnutt certainly sounds a very clever mechanic. And what happened when you got to the delta?

ROSE: _____.

REPORTER: But why couldn't you use the engine?

ROSE: _____.

REPORTER: What a terrible journey! And then in the lake you made your torpedoes and planned your attack.

ROSE: _____.

REPORTER: Well, at least you're not German prisoners of war, Miss Sayer. What are your plans now?

ROSE: _____.

REPORTER: Tomorrow? Oh, that's wonderful! May I come to the wedding and take some photographs?

3 **The reporter wrote a short article based on his interview with Rose. Choose one suitable word to fill each gap.**

Recently Rose Sayer, a British missionary's _____, and her friend Charlie Allnutt, a _____, brought the *African Queen*, an old _____, down the Ulanga into Lake Wittelsbach, _____ they planned to destroy the German _____, *Königin Luise*. It was a very _____ journey. Spengler had done it before, _____ he was in a canoe, which _____ easier to take through rapids. However, _____ two brave people survived. Their propeller _____ and they had to stop to _____ it, and in the delta they _____ to battle through reeds and a _____ swamp. When they finally reached the _____, they fixed their torpedoes onto the _____ and after dark set off to _____ the *Königin Luise*. Sadly, they did _____ succeed. That night there was a _____ storm, and the *African Queen* sank _____ it reached the gunboat.

The attack _____, but the story has a happy _____. On their journey Rose and Charlie _____ in love, and last week they _____ married here in Matadi. We all _____ them a long and happy life _____.

4 **Do all these headlines suit the article above? Explain why some are better than others, and think of some of your own.**

- Love on the River Ulanga
- Goodbye, *African Queen*
- Bravery of Missionary's Sister
- In Spengler's Footsteps
- Attack on the *Königin Luise*
- Torpedo!
- Beaten by a Storm
- Victory on the Lake
- Charlie Finds True Love
- Fighting for Britain

5 **The story ends with Rose and Charlie planning to marry. What do you think happens next? Choose from the ideas below, and write an extra final paragraph to finish the story.**

Rose and Charlie . . .

- get married / don't get married
- live happily together / argue all the time
- have a large family / go looking for adventure / buy a boat
- fall out of love / don't have any money / leave each other

Rose

- goes back to England / stays in Africa / dies of malaria / finds out about Charlie's first wife / marries someone else

Charlie

- is killed in the war / is wounded / runs away to South America / goes back to England / marries someone else

6 **Imagine you are a film director making a film of *The African Queen*. Discuss these questions.**

1 Which stars would you choose to play the parts of Rose and Charlie, and why? (The stars of the famous 1951 film were Katharine Hepburn and Humphrey Bogart.)

2 Would you have a different ending for the story in your film? Choose one of these ideas or think of your own.

- The *African Queen's* torpedoes destroy the *Königin Luise*.
- Rose and Charlie go down with the *African Queen* and are never seen again.
- The Germans shoot Charlie as a spy.
- The film ends with Rose and Charlie's wedding.

ABOUT THE AUTHOR

Cecil Scott Forester was born in Cairo to British parents, in 1899. He went to a private school in London, and studied to be a doctor before becoming a writer. His first successful novel, *Payment Deferred* (1926), set in the First World War, was made into a play and later a film. This was followed by a book about the life of Nelson, and two well-known novels, *Death to the French* (1932) and *The Gun* (1933), about the British war against the French, which took place in Spain and Portugal in the early 1800s. For a time Forester was a script writer in Hollywood, then became a war reporter in the Spanish Civil War and the Second World War. He continued to write novels during the war years, but after 1945 his health became poor, and he moved to California, in the USA. He died in 1966.

Forester's best-known novels are the twelve Hornblower books, which by the time of his death had sold eight million copies. Horatio Hornblower, a young officer in the British navy, was partly based on the life of Britain's most famous admiral, Horatio Nelson, and the novels, all full of accurate historical detail, follow Hornblower's career and adventures.

Forester's other well-known work is *The African Queen* (1935), a classic story of adventure and romance. It became famous as a film directed by John Huston in 1951, starring Katharine Hepburn and Humphrey Bogart (who won an Oscar for his acting in the film).

OXFORD BOOKWORMS LIBRARY

Classics • Crime & Mystery • Factfiles • Fantasy & Horror
Human Interest • Playscripts • Thriller & Adventure
True Stories • World Stories

The OXFORD BOOKWORMS LIBRARY provides enjoyable reading in English, with a wide range of classic and modern fiction, non-fiction, and plays. It includes original and adapted texts in seven carefully graded language stages, which take learners from beginner to advanced level. An overview is given on the next pages.

All Stage 1 titles are available as audio recordings, as well as over eighty other titles from Starter to Stage 6. All Starters and many titles at Stages 1 to 4 are specially recommended for younger learners. Every Bookworm is illustrated, and Starters and Factfiles have full-colour illustrations.

The OXFORD BOOKWORMS LIBRARY also offers extensive support. Each book contains an introduction to the story, notes about the author, a glossary, and activities. Additional resources include tests and worksheets, and answers for these and for the activities in the books. There is advice on running a class library, using audio recordings, and the many ways of using Oxford Bookworms in reading programmes. Resource materials are available on the website <www.oup.com/bookworms>.

The *Oxford Bookworms Collection* is a series for advanced learners. It consists of volumes of short stories by well-known authors, both classic and modern. Texts are not abridged or adapted in any way, but carefully selected to be accessible to the advanced student.

You can find details and a full list of titles in the *Oxford Bookworms Library Catalogue* and *Oxford English Language Teaching Catalogues*, and on the website <www.oup.com/bookworms>.

THE OXFORD BOOKWORMS LIBRARY
GRADING AND SAMPLE EXTRACTS

STARTER • 250 HEADWORDS

present simple – present continuous – imperative –
can/cannot, must – *going to* (future) – simple gerunds …

Her phone is ringing – but where is it?

Sally gets out of bed and looks in her bag. No phone. She looks under the bed. No phone. Then she looks behind the door. There is her phone. Sally picks up her phone and answers it. *Sally's Phone*

STAGE 1 • 400 HEADWORDS

… past simple – coordination with *and*, *but*, *or* –
subordination with *before, after, when, because, so* …

I knew him in Persia. He was a famous builder and I worked with him there. For a time I was his friend, but not for long. When he came to Paris, I came after him – I wanted to watch him. He was a very clever, very dangerous man. *The Phantom of the Opera*

STAGE 2 • 700 HEADWORDS

… present perfect – *will* (future) – *(don't) have to, must not, could* –
comparison of adjectives – simple *if* clauses – past continuous –
tag questions – *ask/tell* + infinitive …

While I was writing these words in my diary, I decided what to do. I must try to escape. I shall try to get down the wall outside. The window is high above the ground, but I have to try. I shall take some of the gold with me – if I escape, perhaps it will be helpful later. *Dracula*

... should, may – present perfect continuous – *used to* – past perfect –
causative – relative clauses – indirect statements ...

Of course, it was most important that no one should see
Colin, Mary, or Dickon entering the secret garden. So Colin
gave orders to the gardeners that they must all keep away
from that part of the garden in future. *The Secret Garden*

STAGE 4 • 1400 HEADWORDS

... past perfect continuous – passive (simple forms) –
would conditional clauses – indirect questions –
relatives with *where/when* – gerunds after prepositions/phrases ...

I was glad. Now Hyde could not show his face to the world
again. If he did, every honest man in London would be proud
to report him to the police. *Dr Jekyll and Mr Hyde*

STAGE 5 • 1800 HEADWORDS

... future continuous – future perfect –
passive (modals, continuous forms) –
would have conditional clauses – modals + perfect infinitive ...

If he had spoken Estella's name, I would have hit him. I was so
angry with him, and so depressed about my future, that I could
not eat the breakfast. Instead I went straight to the old house.
Great Expectations

STAGE 6 • 2500 HEADWORDS

... passive (infinitives, gerunds) – advanced modal meanings –
clauses of concession, condition

When I stepped up to the piano, I was confident. It was as if I
knew that the prodigy side of me really did exist. And when I
started to play, I was so caught up in how lovely I looked that
I didn't worry how I would sound. *The Joy Luck Club*